GODS, GODDESSES and HEROES

MYTHOLOGY from AROUND THE WORLD

text by
Marzia Accatino

illustrations by
Laura Brenlla

CONTENTS

WELCOME!
4

GREECE
6

EGYPT
24

SCANDINAVIA
34

SOUTH ASIA
48

CHINA
56

CENTRAL AMERICA
64

NORTH AMERICA
72

WELCOME, YOUNG FRIEND!

YOU'RE PROBABLY WONDERING WHO I AM. Am I a human? Am I a horse? Well actually I'm neither – I'm a centaur, and my name is Chiron. I'm a professor, and the first thing I want to teach you is that you should never, ever call a creature like me a horse or a nag. There is no worse insult for a centaur! Got it? Glad we've cleared that up.

From the brief lesson I've just given you, you might have guessed that dealing with mythological characters is not easy at all. In this book you'll meet many fantastical animals, deities and mighty monsters with unpredictable natures! In order to survive, you won't need fierce weapons like Thor's hammer or Perseus' shield: what you'll need is knowledge!

I will be your companion and guide on an incredible journey through many parts of the world. I will show you the powers and the weaknesses of the gods, the tricks used by heroes in their adventures, the best ways to approach and befriend strange creatures and the most useful tricks for escaping terrible monsters. If that sounds exciting rather than terrifying, then you're in the right place!

ARE YOU READY?
Turn the page and
let's start our journey!

GREECE

OUR JOURNEY BEGINS in my native land: Greece, where Olympus, home to all the gods of ancient Greece, rises above everything else. We'll climb it together to meet Zeus and his family, before moving on to other exciting adventures. We'll visit places populated by wonderful creatures with magical powers (like Pegasus, a flying horse!). With a bit of luck, and my advice, you'll have all of them by your side when facing the terrible monsters along our way. Don't be scared though! I know a few heroes who can teach you the secrets to becoming invincible!

GODS and GODDESSES

ZEUS

He is the absolute ruler of Olympus, king of all gods and goddesses of the sky.

Be careful when you're in his presence! He has a quick temper and if he gets angry, he wouldn't think twice about using his most dreadful weapon: lightning. His childhood was pretty difficult; as a baby, his mother had to keep him hidden from his father, Cronus, who had a bad habit of devouring his own children.

SACRED ANIMALS: Eagle and bull.

DISTINGUISHING FEATURES: He has the power to transform into anything he wants.

HERA

Hera is the queen of the Olympian gods and wife of Zeus. She is the goddess of women, family and marriage, although ironically her relationship with her husband Zeus is often rocky.

SACRED ANIMALS: Peacock and cow.

DISTINGUISHING FEATURES: Hera can be very jealous and vindictive. You definitely don't want to be on her bad side. She particularly hates Hercules, Zeus' favourite son.

APOLLO

The handsome Apollo loves music and poetry. But his most important – and hardest – mission isn't the pursuit of the arts, but something totally different: he wakes up in the middle of the night to pull the Sun across the sky in his chariot so that a new day can start – every day!

SACRED ANIMALS: Swan and wolf.

DISTINGUISHING FEATURES: He has a twin sister, with whom he briefly crosses paths in the sky each day at dawn and at sunset. Can you guess who she is? It's Artemis, the goddess of the Moon!

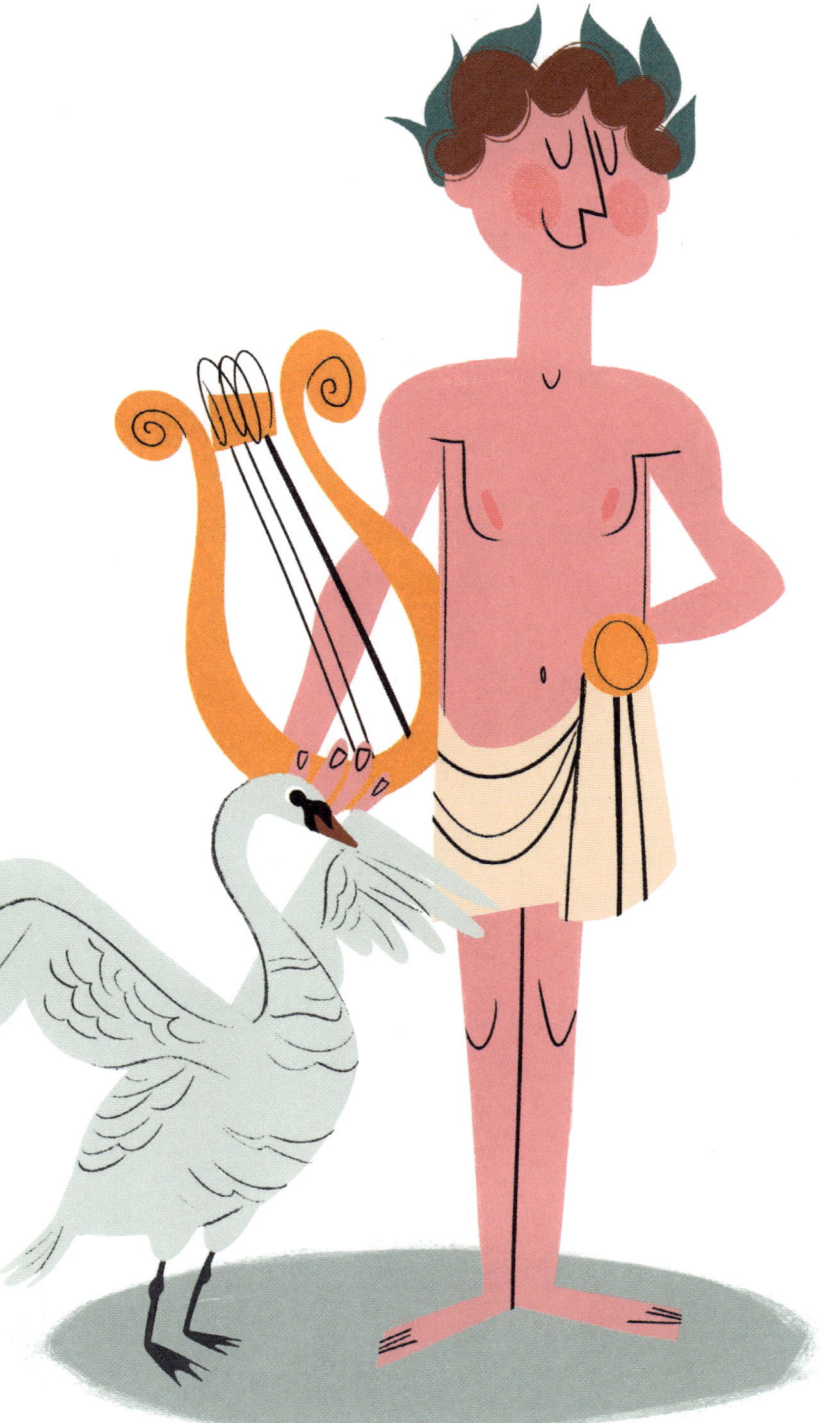

POSEIDON

Zeus's brother, the god of the sea, lives in the depths of the great blue ocean. He is feared by all because he has the power to unleash violent earthquakes and tsunamis. Poseidon is known for being unpredictable and volatile; he can go from being calm to tempestuous very quickly — just like the sea that he governs.

SACRED ANIMALS: Dolphin and horse.

DISTINGUISHING FEATURES: He always carries his three-pronged trident.

APHRODITE

Aphrodite is worshipped as the goddess of beauty and spring. Never question her title as 'the most beautiful of all the gods' — she is very attached to it!

SACRED ANIMALS: Swan and dove.

DISTINGUISHING FEATURES: She is believed to have been born from sea foam and, for this reason, she is the protector of sailors.

ATHENA

She protects the city of Athens — which took its name from hers — and is the goddess of war and wisdom. She is also the goddess of crafts and taught humans how to spin and weave. When she was born, she emerged from her father Zeus' head fully formed!

SACRED ANIMALS: Owl and rooster.

DISTINGUISHING FEATURES: She is often portrayed with a serious and solemn expression and armed with her helmet, spear and indestructible shield called 'aegis'.

PANDORA'S BOX

AS YOU'VE ALREADY SEEN, Greek gods often have some human characteristics. For instance, they can be quite vindictive!

And Zeus is no exception! Read the story of Pandora and judge for yourself.

A LONG TIME AGO, the Titan Prometheus stole the gift of fire from the gods and gave it to mankind. Zeus was furious and came up with a diabolical plan to take revenge and punish humans!

He sent a beautiful woman named Pandora down to Earth with a special gift made by Zeus himself: a box that the woman was ordered to keep closed forever.

However, Pandora was so curious to know what was in the box that she opened it. By doing so, she released all the evils that were previously unknown to man, such as fear and suffering. At the bottom of the box was hope, and Pandora released it into the world as well, in an attempt to be forgiven for her terrible mistake.

HEROES

JASON

Now I want to introduce you to some true Greek heroes! The first is named Jason, famous for being the leader of the Argonauts. This band of valiant heroes was recruited to find the Golden Fleece: the fleece of a ram that was kept inside a sacred forest and protected by a dragon. As you can imagine, carrying out such a venture was no easy task. They even had to face the Harpies, terrible monsters that I will tell you more about soon!

CHARACTERISTICS: It was I, Chiron the centaur, who raised and educated young Jason. And I can say that he was a great pupil!

DISTINGUISHING FEATURES: The name 'Argonauts' comes from the name of their ship, *Argo*.

THESEUS

Theseus is one of the favourite heroes of the people of Athens, where his father, Aegeus, was king. Before Theseus was born, Aegeus hid his sword and a pair of sandals under a big rock. Only when his son was strong enough to lift the rock would he understand who his father was and what destiny awaited him.

CHARACTERISTICS: Because of his great courage and strength, he offered to challenge the Minotaur. I will tell you that story in a moment.

DISTINGUISHING FEATURES: Though he is usually quite the hero, he failed to rescue the goddess Persephone from Hades, God of the underworld. He ended up getting captured himself and had to be rescued by the hero Hercules!

PERSEUS

Son of Zeus and Danae, a princess of Argos, Perseus didn't have it easy from the get-go. A prophecy revealed to his grandfather that the newly born Perseus would eventually kill him, so his grandfather marked him out as an enemy. However, thanks to the protection offered by his divine father, Perseus grew up to be strong and smart. These qualities definitely helped him in his most famous adventure, which I will tell you about shortly: the fight with Medusa.

CHARACTERISTICS: This hero's kit includes: winged sandals, a magical bag, the helmet of invisibility and a mirror-like shield.

DISTINGUISHING FEATURES: Because of his victory over Medusa, he was given the winged horse Pegasus, who became his inseparable companion.

ACHILLES

Have you ever heard the expression 'Achilles' heel'? This now generally refers to a 'weak spot', but do you know where it comes from? When Achilles was born, his mother Thetis dipped him in the River Styx to make him immortal. Unfortunately, she held him by his heel, so the heel didn't receive the protection the rest of his body did. Make sure that you don't share this secret around though…if an enemy should hear of this, Achilles would be in trouble!

CHARACTERISTICS: I've known Achilles since he was a baby. He is an excellent hunter and horse trainer but is also very skilled in the arts: he can play the lyre and sing. Those who know him only as a valiant warrior are always surprised by his grace!

DISTINGUISHING FEATURES: His best friend is Patroclus, a loyal sidekick who never hesitates to go into battle with him.

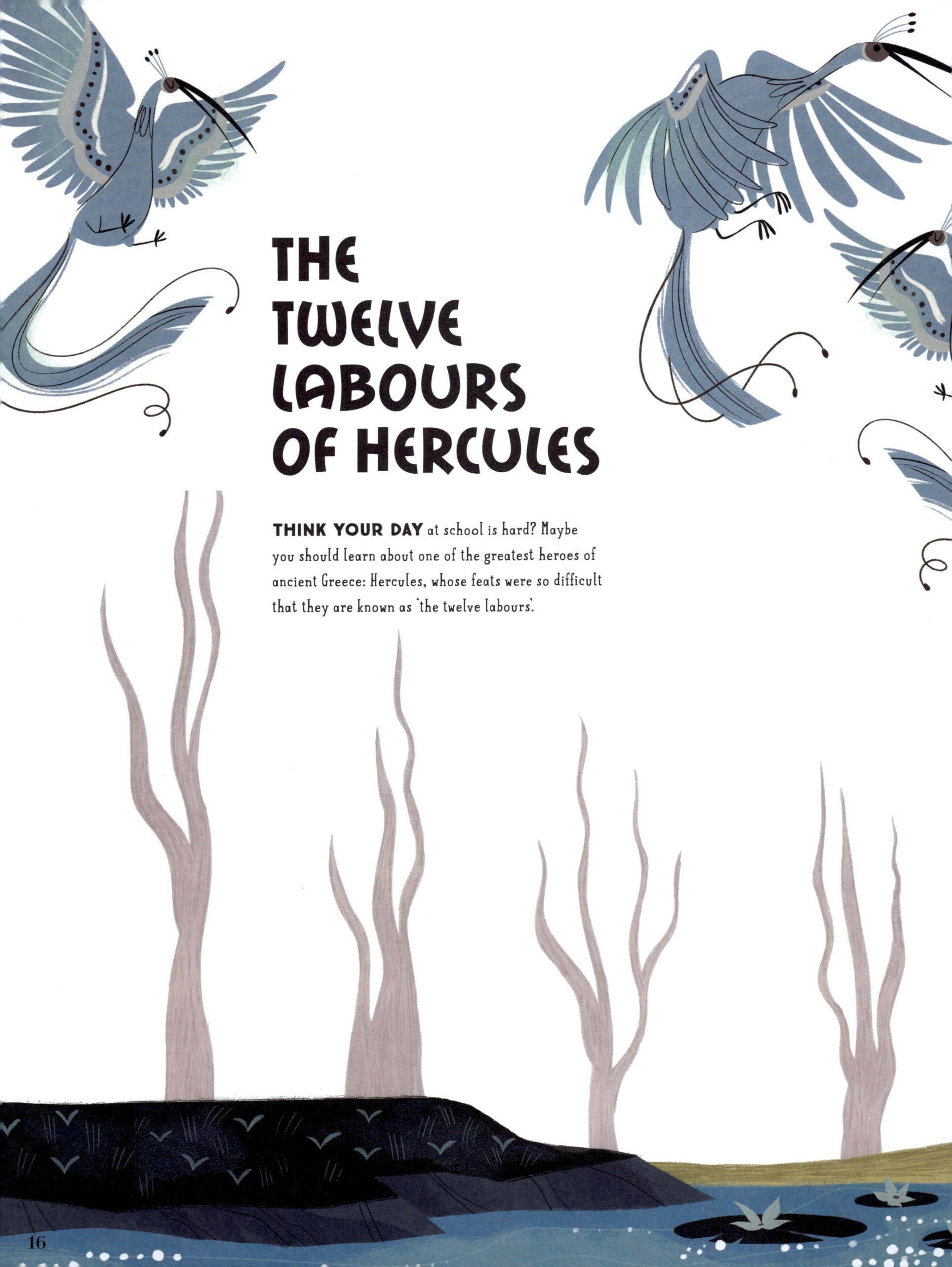

THE TWELVE LABOURS OF HERCULES

THINK YOUR DAY at school is hard? Maybe you should learn about one of the greatest heroes of ancient Greece: Hercules, whose feats were so difficult that they are known as 'the twelve labours'.

HERCULES – a demigod who is the son of Zeus and a human – wanted to gain access to Mt Olympus, home of the gods. To do so, he had to complete a series of twelve tasks, including facing bulls, lions, boars and mythical creatures such as my friends the centaurs and the Amazons, fearsome female warriors.

One of the hardest trials he faced was to defeat the birds of Lake Stymphalia. These birds were monsters with bronze feathers and claws and a sophisticated sense of hearing – a fact which Hercules took advantage of. Because they were in an area that was difficult to reach, Hercules made the birds take off by scaring them with a powerful rattle. Once they were up in the air, it was easier for him to shoot them with his arrows.

Next time you feel tired, think about Hercules' twelve labours and everything will seem easy again!

FANTASTICAL CREATURES

PEGASUS

He's the most famous and elegant winged horse in history. Son of Poseidon, the god of the sea, he has a special bond with water; in fact, he has the power to create new sources of water with a single strike of his hoof! He is most known for the big wings that he sometimes carries folded on his back.

DISTINGUISHING FEATURES: He is a servant of Zeus and transports his thunderbolts; he always knows before anyone else when a storm is approaching.

PHOENIX

Anyone lucky enough to see the phoenix describes it as a big bird similar to an eagle with a plumage coloured in bright red and gold. At dawn you can hear its beautiful melodious singing, so enchanting that even Apollo stops his chariot to listen to it.

DISTINGUISHING FEATURES: Already known to the ancient Egyptians, this bird is also called the 'bird of fire', not just for its bright colours, but also because it is said that it can be reborn from its own ashes. A phoenix could be your eternal friend!

SIRENS

Described as creatures with the body of a bird and the head of a woman, sirens use their beautiful voices to lure sailors to their doom. They tried to tempt poor hero Odysseus in every way possible during his famous journey back to Ithaca. But Odysseus was so wise that he had himself tied to the mast of his ship so he could enjoy their voices without being fatally attracted to them. Quite an extreme solution, yet a good one to keep in mind!

DISTINGUISHING FEATURES: Their singing can tame the winds, if only you can convince them to cooperate, but sirens are not famous for being accommodating.

CENTAURS

My people are easily recognisable: we are each half man and half horse, and extremely good at archery. But I can't say that we are renowned for our good tempers.

DISTINGUISHING FEATURES: Centaurs hate humans, maybe because they have inherited humans' most brutal characteristics to an exaggerated degree.

MONSTERS

MEDUSA

You may be surprised to learn that Medusa wasn't always a monstrous creature with snakes instead of hair. She was once a very beautiful woman who made the mistake of competing with Athena over who was *more* beautiful. Offended and angry, Athena turned her into one of the scariest monsters in all of Greece.

BE CAREFUL BECAUSE... Her gaze has the power to turn anyone who looks at her into stone. So keep your eyes low!

HARPIES

Harpies have the head of a woman and the body of a bird, with big thick wings and strong claws. Their names and their screams bring to mind the fury of sea storms.

BE CAREFUL BECAUSE... Their long, sharp claws are very dangerous weapons. Never let yourself get within their reach!

CHIMERA

This strange creature has the body of a lion with the head of a goat protruding from its back, and a tail that is a snake: the perfect example of a monster!

BE CAREFUL BECAUSE...
It can spit fire out of its mouth and nostrils, and the venom from its tail is fatal!

CYCLOPES

These one-eyed giants are shepherds and live alone in large caves. But you might come across one anyway, like Odysseus and his men did. They were imprisoned by the enormous but not-so-smart Polyphemus.

BE CAREFUL BECAUSE... When the Cyclopes are hungry, they unleash their wild strength – better run away as quickly as you can!

THE MINOTAUR

BRAVE HEROES have already faced some of the most fearful monsters. Learning their stories and the strategies they used to defeat these monsters will help you.

Let's start with the Minotaur....

. . . .

THIS MONSTROUS and ruthless creature, with the body of a man and the head of a bull, was born on the island of Crete.

Knowing how dangerous it was, Minos, the king of Crete, ordered the craftsman Daedalus to build a labyrinth to imprison the monster. But the Minotaur was only contained, not killed. That is until Theseus arrived in Crete and offered to slay the monster! The young hero knew he could count on his own strength, as well as the help of clever Ariadne, King Minos' daughter, who was in love with him.

Ariadne gave Theseus a ball of red thread that he could unravel on the ground so as not to lose his way in the labyrinth. Thanks to her cleverness, Theseus was able to surprise the monster and kill it.

The moral of the story? Sometimes the brain is more useful than muscles!

EGYPT

ANCIENT EGYPT IS WITHOUT DOUBT a fascinating place and the gods who live there are just as fascinating! They have captivating stories to tell, as interesting as their powers. Just be careful not to look too surprised when you meet them, even the god with the head of a jackal!

I will tell you more about him later, but first we must pay tribute to the most important Egyptian deity: Ra, the sun god. Then we'll get to know two rather quarrelsome and vindictive brothers, Osiris and Set. You will also learn about powerful and mesmerising goddesses, like Isis and Hathor, who bring harmony and order to the world. At the end of our journey, you'll find a test waiting for you — something the ancient Egyptians cared about very much — and hopefully you will understand that sometimes scary things are not actually as dangerous as they seem.

But I don't want to give too much away...it's time to start exploring the desert dunes!

GODS and GODDESSES

RA

Bow down before Ra, the most important of all the Egyptian gods! If you don't do it properly, he'll notice because he has power over every part of the world: the Earth, the sky and the underworld. It's impossible to get away from him!

CHARACTERISTICS: Ra is usually portrayed with the head of a falcon and a cobra wrapped around a sun resting on his head.

DISTINGUISHING FEATURES: He travels on two different boats: one to cross the sky during the day, and the other one to descend into the darkness of the underworld.

ISIS

This goddess is beloved for her sweet maternal nature, her wisdom and her knowledge of magic: that's why she is also called 'the great magician'. Her help is even sought by the other gods when they find themselves in trouble. Since word spread that she also has healing powers and can invoke powerful spells to protect against scorpion stings, she no longer gets a moment of peace!

CHARACTERISTICS: Her name in the ancient hieroglyphic writing of Egypt contains a symbol that represents a throne or seat. That's why she is sometimes portrayed seated and with a child in her arms: this is her son, the god Horus.

DISTINGUISHING FEATURES: She has a round sun between two cow horns on her head, and so the cow is her sacred animal.

OSIRIS

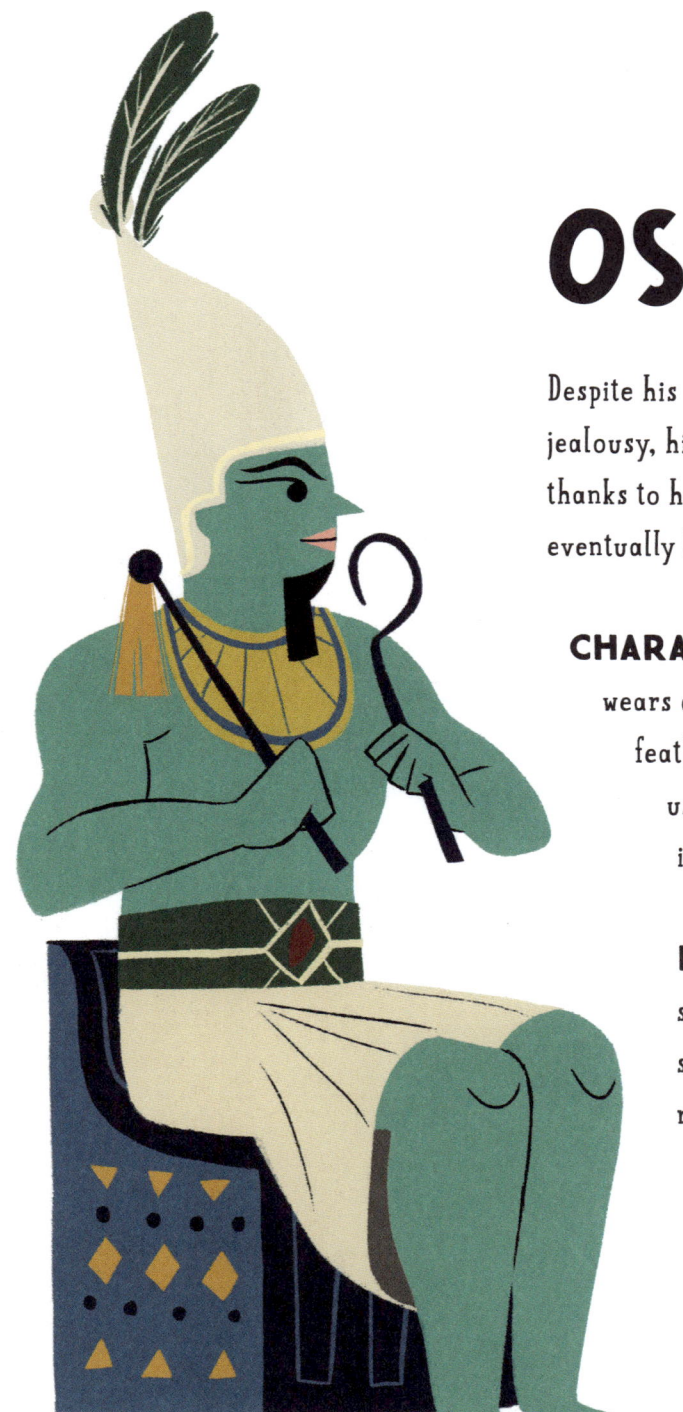

Despite his immense powers, this god didn't have an easy life at all. Blind with jealousy, his brother Set conspired against him and managed to kill him. However, thanks to his wife Isis' magical powers, Osiris was able to come back to life and eventually became the god of the underworld.

CHARACTERISTICS: His appearance is similar to that of a pharaoh: he wears a white crown on his head, typical of royalty, with two long ostrich feathers. He carries a crook and flail against his chest. But the feature that usually attracts the most attention is his green skin! This unusual colour indicates that Osiris is the god of the dead.

DISTINGUISHING FEATURES: I'm sure you've heard of Egyptian mummies: Osiris is sometimes portrayed as a mummy because of his role as the god of the afterlife.

HORUS

This extremely powerful god, son of Isis and Osiris, is able to defeat chaos and bring about order. Horus is also the god of the sky: his left eye represents the Moon; the right one the Sun.

CHARACTERISTICS: Horus can be portrayed in many different ways, but he is most commonly represented as a falcon.

DISTINGUISHING FEATURES: Do you remember the story of Osiris, Horus' father? The young god decided to avenge the murder of his father by Set and confronted his uncle, but he lost an eye in the battle. The 'eye of Horus' has become the most popular and powerful amulet in Egypt.

SET

The god of chaos, disorder, storms and the desert, Set is involved in many matters, most of which are not very pleasant. But he redeems himself by escorting the sun god Ra on his boat across the sky and by helping him to defeat Apep, a giant snake trying to devour Ra.

CHARACTERISTICS: Here is a challenge for you: can you guess what animal Set's face resembles? Difficult, isn't it? Nobody has ever managed to work it out! People have guessed that it's a jackal, a donkey, or even a fennec (a type of fox that lives in the desert) but we now generally just call it the 'Set animal'.

DISTINGUISHING FEATURES: His skin is red, like the sand of the desert over which he reigns.

ANUBIS

This god is the first protector of the underworld. Anubis battled Set, who transformed himself into a leopard. When Anubis won he branded Set – and it's said that's how the leopard got its spots!

CHARACTERISTICS: His head is like that of a jackal – a nocturnal animal that, although usually considered scary, was actually worshipped by the ancient Egyptians.

DISTINGUISHING FEATURES: Anubis's head is black as silt – the fertile soil that the River Nile produces after every flood – as a symbol of rebirth.

HATHOR

She is one of the most beloved goddesses and is associated with joyous and fun occasions. She is the goddess of love, beauty, music and dance. The Egyptians also entrusted Hathor with a very important task: protecting the sources of the River Nile.

CHARACTERISTICS: She is sometimes portrayed as a cow – an animal considered a symbol of femininity – often with cow ears as well. On her head is a round sun between two cow horns, or sometimes between two feathers.

DISTINGUISHING FEATURES: She cannot be parted from her partner, Ra. He becomes very sad when Hathor, who is the goddess of joy, is not there.

NUT

Nut, the goddess of the sky, is depicted as a giant woman who supports the weight of the skies on her back. She's very strong! Nut is married to Geb, the god of the Earth.

CHARACTERISTICS: Nut controls the gift of rebirth. For example, every day at sunset, Nut swallows the Sun, then gives birth to it again each morning.

DISTINGUISHING FEATURES: Her hair is depicted as a delicate rain that bathes the Earth.

SACRED ANIMALS

SCARAB BEETLE

The scarab may look like a normal insect to you, but to the ancient Egyptians it symbolised the Sun and brought good luck. Here's why: the scarab produces small balls of dung that it then rolls between its legs. When observing this curious behaviour, the ancient Egyptians compared it to the movement of the Sun across the sky.

DID YOU KNOW? The scarab beetle is also a symbol of rebirth, and this belief comes from another observation of its behaviour. The beetle is born from eggs laid in a ball of dung. The ancient Egyptians believed this made the scarab exactly like the Sun, which is reborn every day at dawn.

CAT

Cats are held in such high regard in Egypt that they have their own personal goddess! The cat is a sacred animal and is protected by Bastet, the cat-headed goddess.

DID YOU KNOW? Many ancient Egyptian women wore an amulet featuring Bastet surrounded by her cats as a lucky charm.

IBIS

With thin legs and an elongated beak, the ibis chose the banks of the River Nile as its home. The ancient Egyptians valued them very highly; in fact they often mummified them, a process Egyptians believed help secure a happy afterlife.

DID YOU KNOW? The ibis has become a symbol of intelligence and wisdom and therefore represents mathematics and writing. Thoth, the god who presides over these subjects, is portrayed with the head of an ibis.

THE WEIGHING OF THE HEART

FOR THE ANCIENT EGYPTIANS, the underworld was very important. Life after death was seen almost as a continuation of life on Earth.

HOWEVER, IN ORDER to gain access to this world, you must first pass a test: the weighing of the heart. And that's where Anubis, the jackal god, comes in. He escorts the deceased in Osiris's Hall of Judgement and places their heart on a scale. Its weight is compared to an ostrich feather, symbol of Ma'at, the goddess of justice and truth. Thoth, the god of writing, writes down the verdict: if the heart is as light as the feather, and therefore sincere and free from the weight of bad deeds, Osiris declares that the deceased is allowed to live forever in the underworld!

SCANDINAVIA

WRAP UP WARM because an adventure in cold and distant lands awaits us! Where do you think we're going?

Here is a hint: the Sun behaves differently in these places! It disappears for months on end, leaving everything and everyone in darkness, and at other times it doesn't set for weeks. That alone should tell you that the lands we are about to explore are full of magic and legends. And you'd be right: the myths of Norway, Sweden, Finland and Iceland are filled with giants, fantastical animals, mighty warriors and brave horsemen. Their fates are controlled by several gods — lords of the sky who all descend from the great Odin, the ruler of Asgard. Asgard, the home of the gods, is a fortress filled with grand halls covered in gold. In the largest hall, called Valhalla, the gods welcome heroes who fell in battle.

Here we will meet Thor with his famous hammer, the trickster Loki, and also some beautiful goddesses, like Freya and Frigg. You will discover that even a wild boar can be as valiant as a horse with the help of a little magic, and that the Nordic people have learnt not to trust the sea because it can hide huge and dreadful monsters.

What are we waiting for? Let's go!

GODS and GODDESSES

ODIN

The ruler of Asgard is Odin, father to all the gods and goddesses of northern Europe. It's not easy to recognise him, because he has the ability to change his form: he can appear as a terrible and ruthless warrior ready to fight his enemies, but he can also disguise himself as a wanderer who walks the Earth wrapped up in his cloak.

CHARACTERISTICS:
Odin is renowned for his wisdom, which comes from being the oldest of all the gods and the creator of the world. His infinite wisdom allows him, among other things, to know the destiny of all humans.

DISTINGUISHING FEATURES:
He never parts from his spear, called Gungnir, or from Sleipnir, his loyal eight-legged horse.

THOR

I bet you've already heard of Thor, the god of thunder, lightning and storms, who also has the power to control the rain. While his father Odin is the leader of all the gods, Thor is the god of men and the protector of humanity, which he defends with the help of a loyal friend: his famous and heavy hammer, Mjöllnir!

CHARACTERISTICS: He has a strong and powerful physique and long hair, but he also has a heart of gold. Thor is much loved by the people.

DISTINGUISHING FEATURES: Along with his hammer, Thor also carries a magical belt that can double the strength of anyone wearing it.

HEIMDALLR

Because he only needs a few minutes of sleep to regain his strength, Heimdallr is the perfect guardian of a very special place: the Bifröst, the rainbow bridge that joins the Earth with Asgard, home of the gods.

CHARACTERISTICS: His senses are highly developed: he can hear the slightest noise, like the sound of grass growing, and he can see what happens beyond the horizon.

DISTINGUISHING FEATURES: He has a very powerful horn called Gjallarhorn, which can be heard from every corner of the world.

LOKI

Be very careful when you find yourself in Loki's presence. He is renowned for his cunning and could easily help you get out of trouble, but he is also known as 'the god of deception'. He is a troublemaker and sometimes enjoys playing cruel pranks. In short, be on your guard!

CHARACTERISTICS: Loki has dark hair. This trickster also loves jokes!

DISTINGUISHING FEATURES: One of Loki's symbols is fire. Just like fire, he can be both benevolent and destructive.

SIF

This beautiful goddess, Thor's wife, is the protector of wheat, harvest and the Earth. Sif is one of the Valkyries, female warriors who are very hard to beat in battle! I will tell you more about them in a bit....

CHARACTERISTICS: You will often see her holding a sheaf of wheat. Humans invoke her help to convince Thor to let rain fall on their fields, so they might have rich and abundant harvests. She has been seen transforming herself into a swan, the Valkyries' sacred animal.

DISTINGUISHING FEATURES: She has beautiful, long golden hair. This did not escape the notice of Loki and, some time ago, he decided to pull a prank and chop it off while she was asleep. It was only Thor's fury that convinced him to return the stolen locks!

FREYA

She is the goddess of beauty, fertility and love, although we can't say that she is very lucky in matters of love! Her husband Óðr often abandons her to make long journeys. She is also the goddess of battle and rides a boar into the fray.

CHARACTERISTICS: Freya has long, golden hair and is known to be very beautiful. Determined and brave, she is one of the fearsome Valkyries.

DISTINGUISHING FEATURES: You can spot her while she crosses the sky on a chariot pulled by two cats, her favourite animals.

FREYR

He is considered to be the god of love, like his twin sister Freya, although he is not as attractive as she is. He can be recognised by his long hair and scruffy beard. Sometimes his clothes are stained with green, because he loves living in the woods and sleeping out on the grass.

CHARACTERISTICS: When he was still a newborn, he and his twin sister were given to Odin.

DISTINGUISHING FEATURES: His best friend is Gullinbursti. Are you curious to know who that is? You'll find out very soon!

THE MYTH OF DAGR AND NÓTT

AS FAR AS I CAN TELL, every culture has tried to come up with an explanation for the cycle of day and night.

· ·

For the Norse people it is all down to the god Dagr and his mother, the goddess Nótt. She is the daughter of a giant and has long, black hair. From her encounter with Dellingr, the god of dawn, a beautiful baby came into the world. He was blonde and bright like his father, and his name, Dagr, means 'day'.

Dagr and Nótt received a chariot and a horse each as a gift from Odin. The horses are called 'shining mane' and 'frost mane'.

These horses are so powerful that they can cross the whole sky in twelve hours. Nótt comes first, bringing the darkness and cold of night and the morning dew with her, then Dagr chases her, and his horse's hair is so bright that it lights up the air and the Earth.

HEROES

STARKAD

This legendary hero had a turbulent childhood! He is the son of a giant but was raised in the court of a king. Because of the incredible strength he has possessed ever since he was a child, every leader wanted to have him in their army rather than risk facing him as an enemy. When he grew up, he found protection and hospitality in several kingdoms, but he eventually made so many enemies that he decided to board a ship and set sail for the north.

DISTINGUISHING FEATURES:
Starkad's appearance used to be quite striking: he was born with eight arms! But Thor, Starkard's rival, made sure that he only had two — by cutting off the other six!

SIGURD

A distant relative of Odin, Sigurd was raised by a dwarf blacksmith called Regin. Regin encouraged him to face the dragon Fafnir to prove his courage. Our hero faced the scary creature and managed to defeat it after a terrible battle. Later, Sigurd cooked and ate the dragon's heart. This gave him the ability to understand the language of birds, who warned him that Regin planned to betray him.

DISTINGUISHING FEATURES: When he slayed Fafnir, Sigurd took possession of the dragon's most important power: invulnerability! However, he still has a weak spot: a leaf had landed on his neck, leaving a small portion of his skin unprotected.

SVIPDAGR

This hero was charged with rescuing a maiden about whom he knew nothing except her name: Menglöð. To accomplish this task (which turned out to be a rather complex venture), he asked for his dead mother's help, and her ghost cast nine spells to accompany him on his journey. When he arrived at Menglöð's castle, Svipdagr had to face a battle that was very different from the ones the Norse heroes were used to. The fight with the keeper of the castle was one of riddles! After solving all of them, Svipdagr finally met Menglöð, who fell in love with him at first sight!

DISTINGUISHING FEATURES: Watching Svipdagr approach the castle, Menglöð's dogs started wagging their tails and jumping around happily: this convinced Menglöð that our hero was indeed the one!

FANTASTICAL CREATURES

RATATOSKR

Ratatoskr the squirrel lives on Yggdrasill, the most important tree in the kingdom. His job is to carry messages between Níðhöggr, the gigantic dragon-snake who lives among the roots of the tree, and the great eagle that lives on top of the tree. That's why you see him running up and down the tree trunk day and night!

DID YOU KNOW? Ratatoskr can move at lightning speed. One of the meanings of his name is 'the travelling tooth'.

NÍÐHÖGGR

The dragon-snake that lives at the roots of Yggdrasill isn't very nice at all. When it's not sending angry messages through Ratatoskr to the eagle at the top of the sacred tree, it gnaws nervously at the roots, risking cutting it down. It's no coincidence that its name means 'one who strikes with hate'.

DID YOU KNOW? The sacred tree Yggdrasill is believed to support all the worlds with its branches, including the world where the gods live. It would be a huge problem if Níðhöggr managed to destroy its roots!

HAFGUFA

The appearance of this gigantic sea monster will surprise you – when it rises up to the surface of the water at night, it looks like an island or a huge pile of rocks. Men have learned how to recognise it even during the day, because this monster feeds not only on whales but also on ships and fishermen. Better keep away from it!

DID YOU KNOW? In ancient Icelandic, the name Hafgufa means 'sea-steam' – maybe inspired by the stories told by fishermen who reported having seen the creature emerge from an unusual fog.

GULLINBURSTI

This magical boar is Freyr's most loyal friend and pulls his chariot. It can run faster than a horse, both in the sky and on water, and during the day as well as at night. Do you know why it's unbeatable even in the dark? Gullinbursti is covered with golden bristles that are so bright that they can light up the night sky.

DID YOU KNOW? Gullinbursti was created by the dwarves, a people with incredible magical knowledge, who can create fantastical creatures and make unbeatable weapons, such as Thor's hammer.

THE RIDE OF THE VALKYRIES

CAN YOU HEAR THAT NOISE?
Where are all those ravens coming from? Oh, I see! The Valkyries are coming; there must be a battle going on somewhere! What's that you're saying? You've never heard of them? Let me tell you everything....

THE VALKYRIES ARE BRAVE and beautiful women who ride flying horses. They are on a mission on behalf of Odin: their task is to fly to battlefields – which are quite common in Norse lands, as you've seen – to choose the most valiant slain warriors and take them to Valhalla, the big hall in Asgard, Odin's kingdom. The Valkyries' chosen soldiers have to undergo tough training to prepare for Ragnarök, the battle that will take place at the end of the world, when they will have to fight by their king's side.

SOUTH ASIA

WE ARE ABOUT HALFWAY through our journey, but I still have so much to tell you!

We are about to venture into South Asia where the sacred River Ganges flows and the tallest mountains in the world rise up into the sky, the home to many deities. Some dieties are so intertwined with each another that they can't exist on their own. They are Brahma, the creator of the Universe, Shiva the destroyer and Vishnu the preserver. Alongside them are some wonderful female goddesses, such as the benevolent Parvati, Shiva's wife.

We will also meet interesting mythical figures, such as the Nagas, half human and half snake, and the Garudas, bird-like people. However, you shouldn't let these powerful creatures scare you, for they actually love humans dearly and desire only happiness for you.

It's time to start our journey!

DEITIES

BRAHMA

This god is the creator of the Universe and has four heads, which each face one of the four compass points. Thanks to this, he can watch the whole Universe: nothing escapes his sight! You can see him riding through the sky on the back of Hamsa, the wise goose from which he is inseparable.

CHARACTERISTICS: In his hands Brahma carries several highly symbolic objects, including a water pot, which symbolises the creation of the Universe from water.

DISTINGUISHING FEATURES: According to legend, Brahma was asleep for eons inside an egg. When the shell broke, the Universe emerged: with the upper half of the shell Brahma created the sky, and with the lower half, he created the Earth.

SHIVA

The story of this deity is very long, but I'll try to sum it up in a few words. A long time ago, Shiva was known by the name Rudra and had a really bad temper! He was very grumpy most of the time and could only keep his anger under control for brief periods, during which he would be addressed as Shiva. Luckily, over time his good side took over, and eventually his name changed to Shiva permanently.

CHARACTERISTICS: Shiva can take many different forms: he can be portrayed as the king of dance, or as a ferocious warrior or sitting cross-legged immersed in meditation.

DISTINGUISHING FEATURES: Shiva's family is as famous as he is: I will introduce you to his son Ganesha and his wife Parvati, the goddess of the mountains.

VISHNU

Vishnu is the god who cares the most about the fate of the world and humankind. He acts as a link between the deities and the people and tries to keep the forces of the world in balance, making sure that good always triumphs over evil.

CHARACTERISTICS: Vishnu has four arms and each of his hands carries a different symbolic object: a chakra (wheel) that represents the circle of time, a club he used to defeat a powerful demon, a shell whose sound will make enemies flee and a lotus flower, the symbol of enlightenment.

DISTINGUISHING FEATURES: He is known by many names – almost a thousand different ones – and they are all collected in a book. One name in particular, 'Cakravartin' means 'ruler of the Universe'.

PARVATI

Parvati is the daughter of the lord of the Himalayas. The Himalayas are the tallest mountains in the world, also known as 'the home of snow'. She is the wife of Shiva, whose heart she won with the help of Kama, the god of love. To make Shiva fall in love with Parvati, Kama shot him with an arrow, just like Eros, the Greek god of love, does where I come from.

CHARACTERISTICS: Parvati has many forms. Sometimes she is shown in her warrior form, known as Durga, riding a tiger into battle!

DISTINGUISHING FEATURES: Parvati looks very delicate, like the lotus flower that she often holds in her hands. She is worshipped by women, especially the married ones, who call on her to protect their husbands.

DIVINE BEINGS

MAKARA

This sea creature is sometimes described as a crocodile or an elephant with the head of an elephant and a body of a fish. He is immensely powerful. Makara is connected to the water, and represents water's vital energy. He also acts as a vehicle for the sea god Varuna, and Ganga, the goddess of the Ganges River.

DID YOU KNOW? You will often find images of Makara on the doors of houses or carved onto the walls of Indian temples, because he is thought to bring happiness and good luck.

GARUDAS

Garudas are half-bird, half-human creatures, with wings and beaks similar to that of parrots. Their main occupation is to defeat the Nagas, half-snake, half-human creatures that I will tell you more about shortly. Garudas also have the magical power to heal the wounds caused by the Nagas' bites.

DID YOU KNOW? These creatures get their name from their most celebrated leader, Garuda, who is Vishnu's vehicle. This god is often portrayed riding on the back of this mythical bird.

NAGA

These semidivine creatures look like snake people. They live underwater, on the bottoms of rivers and lakes, alongside treasures that they must guard. They require no extra protection because they look so scary that nobody dares to approach and challenge them.

DID YOU KNOW? The Nagas can morph into human form. Be careful, you may not recognise them!

GANESHA

Ganesha has the body of a human and the head of an elephant, but with only one intact tusk. He is a very wise and intelligent god, and the protector of writers. He is known for removing obstacles and barriers in people's lives.

DID YOU KNOW? Ganesha uses a mouse as his vehicle, which symbolises the overcoming of obstacles.

THE STORY OF GARUDA, THE TORTOISE AND THE ELEPHANT

THERE IS SOMETHING ELSE that you should know about the leader Garuda. One of the many nicknames of this fantastical being is 'bearer of heavy weight'. Do you want to know why?

O**NE DAY,** overcome with hunger, Garuda captured and killed a gigantic tortoise and a large elephant. Afterwards he was so exhausted that he decided to eat his meal on the branch of a nearby tree. But there were some tiny creatures on that very branch, which was beginning to snap under the weight. They were Brahma's sages, and would definitely fall to the ground and be hurt if Garuda didn't leave in time. To save them, Garuda used all his remaining strength to lift the branch, along with the elephant and the tortoise, carrying them away with his wings.

CHINA

WELCOME TO EAST ASIA and, in particular, welcome to China! This country is home to many incredible ancient gods, goddeses and fantastical creatures. But all of them have one thing in common: they all originated from the god Pangu, who created the wind with his breath, the thunder with his voice, the Sun and the Moon with his eyes and the mountains with his powerful body. You will also meet the four guardian animals, including the white tiger and the black tortoise, who helped Pangu in his heroic venture.

Before starting our journey, we need to pay respect to the Sanxing: Fu Xing, Lu Xing and Shou Xing, three very popular gods who symbolise prosperity, status and longevity. With their blessings on our side, I'm sure we will be safe! Now we're ready to start our adventure into the world of Chinese mythology.

GODS and GODDESSES

CHANG'E

Lovely Chang'e is the goddess of the Moon, and her story is truly fascinating. She is married to Hou Yi, one of the best archers in the world. Because of his skills, the Chinese emperor asked Hou Yi to shoot down nine of the ten suns that were scorching the Earth and preventing night from falling. As a reward, he was given the precious potion of immortality. Tempted by its fragrance, Chang'e drank the potion and her body immediately became so light that she lifted up off the ground! Her flight ended on the Moon, where the goddess still lives today.

CHARACTERISTICS: Each month, when there is a full moon, Chang'e waits to be reunited with her husband, who has made his home on the Sun so that he might stay close to his beloved wife.

DISTINGUISHING FEATURES: Keeping Chang'e company on the Moon is Yutu, a lunar rabbit with magical powers who is able to make the potion of immortality.

FEILIAN

Meet the god of the wind. As you can imagine, he's quite the turbulent type, but luckily Hou Yi, the archer and husband of Chang'e, keeps him in check. Can you imagine what chaos might ensue if the god of the wind were allowed to do anything he wanted?

CHARACTERISTICS: You can see him in his human form, as an old bearded man holding a fan; or in his animal form, as a winged bird, with the head of a deer and the tail of a snake.

DISTINGUISHING FEATURES: As well as the god, Feilian, there also is a goddess of the wind, called Feng Po Po. She rides through the clouds on the back of a tiger.

PANGU

In creation mythology, the Universe originated from an egg that had contained all the cosmic forces for over 18,000 years. Eventually, Pangu emerged from it, the first living creature and creator of all things. The powerful Pangu swung his giant axe and divided the shell, creating the Earth and the sky. To tell you the truth, he didn't actually do it all by himself; he was helped by a few mythical animals, which we will talk about shortly.

CHARACTERISTICS: Pangu has horns on his head and wears animal fur.

DID YOU KNOW? After creating the Earth and the sky, some say Pangu died and different parts of him became pieces of the world.

SANXING

Do you remember that at the beginning of our journey to China, we invoked the Sanxing? Here is some more information about these deities. Fu Xing, Lu Xing and Shou Xing are also nicknamed 'the three stars' and often travel together. They are much loved by the people and are believed to bring happiness and good luck.

CHARACTERISTICS: Lu Xing is accompanied by a deer, Fu Xing by a bat and Shou Xing has two sacred animals: a crane and a turtle.

DISTINGUISHING FEATURES: As you can see from his long white beard, Shou Xing is the oldest of the three. He is much loved by his people, who ask him for a long and happy life. He possesses an extremely rare fruit: the golden peach of immortality, which, according to legend, ripens every 3000 years.

FANTASTICAL CREATURES

ARE YOU READY TO MEET THE FOUR GUARDIANS?
Each of them represents one season of the year and the four cardinal directions, so why are there five in total? Let me tell you!

BLACK TORTOISE

The black tortoise is the guardian of winter and the North. A symbol of wisdom and long life, it is considered to be a lucky charm. It is said that the tortoise's legs were cut off to support the sky.

VERMILION BIRD

The colour of this animal might help you guess what element it represents. That's right, fire! With its bright and colourful feathers, the vermilion bird is the symbol of summer and of the richness and variety of nature. It also represents the South.

WHITE TIGER

Meet the guardian of the West and autumn. Its element is metal. This animal also represents the god of war and defends the emperor's army during battles.

YELLOW DRAGON

The mystery of the fifth animal is finally revealed! It is the Yellow Dragon, guardian of the centre of the Earth and symbol of the constant and unalterable cycle of the four seasons.

AZURE DRAGON

This enormous dragon is the symbol of the East and of spring. It is associated with two colours: blue and green. Its element is wood, and it has the power to control the rain, the rivers and the sea.

NÜWA'S CREATION OF THE WORLD

AS I TOLD YOU EARLIER, Pangu created the world and the whole Universe, but it was the goddess Nüwa who infused all the creatures of the Earth with the essence of life. Get comfortable, I'm about to tell you a very, very old story.

ALTHOUGH PANGU had created mountains, rivers and plants, the goddess Nüwa felt very lonely on Earth. One day, suddenly, an idea came to her and she thought of creating animals to have some company. On the first day, she created chickens; on the second, dogs; on the third, pigs; on the fourth, sheep; on the fifth, cows; and on the sixth, horses. But all those creatures were not enough to drive away her loneliness, so on the seventh day, while she was looking at her reflection in the waters of the Yellow River, she took some clay and started modelling it with her hands, creating a living creature that slowly started to resemble her more than any other creature before. Once she had finished, Nüwa realised that she had created a human being. Excited, she carried on modelling more and more men and women, who started dancing happily all around her. And humanity was born!

CENTRAL AMERICA

EVEN THOUGH YOU CAN SEE stone pyramids in the distance, we are far from Egypt! We're approaching Central America to explore the myths and the gods of two civilisations: the Mayans and the Aztecs. We will talk about their lands, where corn grows strong and abundant thanks to the help of the god Yum Kaax, the Chaac — gods of rain — and their frog friends.

With a bit of luck, we will encounter the colourful quetzal and the playful howler monkey, both forest creatures with unexpectedly strong powers! And I will tell you about the gift given by Quetzalcoatl, the feathered snake, to mankind...or maybe I'll make you taste it!

GODS and GODDESSES

CHAAC OR TLALOC

In a country with such a hot climate, you can easily understand why the most beloved gods are the ones that control and govern the rains. They are called Chaac by the Mayans and Tlaloc by the Aztecs, but they are always four gods, placed at the four compass points. Chaac makes rain by throwing snakes and axes into the clouds (or sometimes by crying tears of sadness).

CHARACTERISTICS: They are enormous and have long noses that resemble an elephant's trunk!

DISTINGUISHING FEATURES: Chaac is great friends with frogs; if you are patient, I will soon tell you why.

YUM KAAX

Because corn is such an important food for the Mayans, it was assigned its very own god for protection! Yum Kaax makes sure that the corn plants grow healthy and strong and grants protection to the harvest from summer to winter. He is also the protector of wild plants and animals.

CHARACTERISTICS: Yum Kaax is portrayed with corncobs that seem to be growing out of his hair.

DISTINGUISHING FEATURES: Yum Kaax grants his protection especially to those farmers who dedicate prayers to him and burn incense as an offering during the sowing and harvesting seasons.

TOCI OR IXCHEL

Now I want to tell you about a goddess that the Aztecs call Toci and the Mayans call Ixchel; she represents the creative force of nature and is considered the mother of all deities. She is a warrior, but also a healer. She is always present when a baby comes into the world, because her task is to protect mothers and their children.

CHARACTERISTICS: Do you know that snakes swallow their prey whole? For this reason, the Mayans believe that snakes possess a magical power and they worship them. Ixchel wears a snake on her head, to signify the coiled serpent and its healing abilities.

DISTINGUISHING FEATURES: Her most recognisable attributes are her ears. They are shaped like those of a jaguar!

CHALCHIUHTLICUE

This Aztec goddess protects the waters of rivers, lakes and oceans. She is always portrayed sitting among green and blue waters that surround her like a long flowing skirt. She is also associated with fertility and childbirth.

CHARACTERISTICS: She often wears beautiful and colourful headpieces.

DISTINGUISHING FEATURES: She created a flood that engulfed the whole Earth, and turned those who were not in her grace into fish. It also destroyed the fourth sun.

FANTASTICAL CREATURES

HOWLER MONKEY

Don't be surprised if you see a small ink pot between this primate's paws: the howler monkey protects all the arts, like writing, sculpting and music.

They say that the howler monkey uses its drawings to serve as a messenger between humans and gods. Apart from being funny and a bit naughty, it is believed to be very wise.

QUETZAL

This beautiful bird is sacred for both the Mayans and the Aztecs. What makes it so special is its brilliant colours, ranging from bright green on its head and back to bright red on its chest. The male can be recognised by the tuft of feathers on its head, which is similar to a mohawk.

DID YOU KNOW? For the Mayans, only very important people have the privilege of wearing quetzal feathers on their heads: such precious headwear is a symbol of prestige and freedom.

FROGS

The Mayans and the Aztecs think that frogs are the messengers of the rain gods. In fact, their croaking is seen as a sign that rain is coming. Sometimes I've seen children squatting down and imitating the sound of a frog to call on the gods and ask for rain.

QUETZAL-COATL

The name of this Aztec god, who is worshipped as the god of the sky, sounds a bit like a tongue-twister! It means 'snake with quetzal feathers' but sometimes Quetzalcoatl takes the form of the 'wind spirit': a man wearing a black-and-red mask similar to a bird's beak.

DID YOU KNOW? Some say that Quetzalcoatl invented books and the calendar. But he also gave humans another great gift that I'm sure you'll appreciate: the cacao plant, which makes chocolate!

THE LEGEND OF CORN

IF YOU LIKE POPCORN, you will certainly be interested to hear the story of how it was created. First of all, you need to know that the Mayans and the Aztecs consider corn an extremely important crop. They believe it is protected by the young god Yum Kaax, who humans call on to bring rich and abundant harvests. However, the first creatures to discover corn were not men....

ACCORDING TO LEGEND, there were once hundreds of corncobs hidden beneath a mountain. The first creatures to discover them were ants: they dug a tunnel under the mountain and, with patience and determination, they started to move the corn out, one kernel at a time. When people discovered how tasty the corn was, they asked the gods to help them get all the corn out from underneath the mountain at once. The gods solved the problem by firing a lightning bolt onto the mountain and toasting some of the kernels. Maybe that's how popcorn was created!

NORTH AMERICA

DEAR FRIEND, we have reached the final leg of our journey. This time I will take you to North America to learn about the Indigenous peoples who have been living here since ancient times. There are many Native American tribes with different belief systems. We will learn about the oral traditions of some tribes. Many of the stories are about nature and animals, for which the Indigenous peoples have a profound respect.

I hope you are not afraid of coyotes, as we will encounter this trickster figure! Do you know, for instance, the coyote gave the gift of fire to humans in the Navajo, Akimel O'odham and Cheyenne oral traditions? Or that the crow gave daylight to the Inuit people? You're about to find out how — and more!

LET'S GO!

SACRED FIGURES

THE CREATOR

There is nothing greater or more powerful than the Creator. Tribes have different names for it. For example, to the Cherokee it is called Unetlanvhi, to the Sioux it is Wakan Tanka and among the Algonquian-speaking people it is Gitchi-Manitou. Across tribes, though, the Creator's characteristics are similar. The Creator is reflected in the creatures of the Universe, in the changing seasons, in the cycle of night and day, and in the movement of celestial bodies, such as the Moon and the stars. It reminds Native peoples that humankind is just one piece of the Universe.

CHARACTERISTICS: The Creator has no human form; it is a force that connects all living things and has powers far beyond any human understanding.

DISTINGUISHING FEATURES: In many oral traditions, the Creator created the land that was given to the Indigenous peoples.

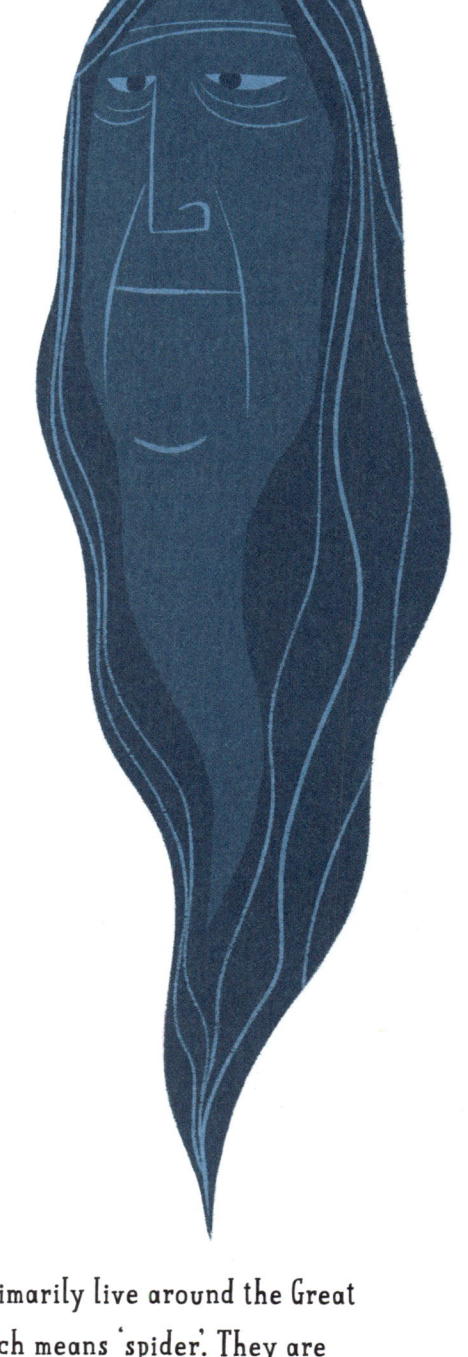

DREAM CATCHER

This sacred object originated with the Ojibwe tribe who primarily live around the Great Lakes. The Ojibwe call dream catchers, 'asabikeshiinh', which means 'spider'. They are made of wood bent into a circular shape. Leather laces, sinew or thread are intertwined to create a web-like design at the centre. The dream catcher's purpose is to catch and trap nightmares and allow good dreams to continue through. Other tribes use them as well, such as the Lakota and Haudenosaunee.

CHARACTERISTICS: The flexible willow stick that forms the hoop represents the circle of life, while the web inside symbolises the Universe.

DID YOU KNOW? Dream catchers are crafted in a series of ceremonial steps. They are not universal among Native cultures, but non-Indigenous cultures have appropriated, or wrongfully taken and used, this symbol without a full understanding of, or respect for, its meaning.

TRICKSTERS

There are many trickster figures across Native American lore. Tricksters can cause all sorts of mischief! They often take the shape of animals, such as the spider, raven and rabbit, but they can take on a human form if needed. I am going to tell you more about the coyote.

CHARACTERISTICS: Coyote is part human and part animal, taking whichever form works for his purposes. He is very clever and is at the centre of oral traditions, including those from the Navajo, Akimel O'odham and Cheyenne tribes. One well-known story is about the theft of fire. It is said that Coyote found the only remote tribe that had discovered how to light a fire and stole one spark from it. Coyote then brought the fire to all the other tribes in the land by organising a relay race with other animals.

DISTINGUISHING FEATURES: Not all of the coyote's character traits are appreciated by humans. His clever and conniving nature not only lands others in trouble but also himself!

TOTEM

The tribes of the Pacific Northwest created monuments known as totem poles, which are often made of cedar wood. The name derives from the Ojibwe word 'Ototeman' and can have different names across languages and tribes. In the Haida language, the word is 'Gyáa'aang'. Totem poles are carved for many purposes. Some document a family's lineage or history, but they do not tell stories; instead they record events and legends connected to a certain household or tribe. Only those already familiar with what is being recorded would fully understand it.

CHARACTERISTICS: There are many different types of totem poles. Some are used to mark graves, memorialise the dead, support a home or welcome people, among other purposes.

DISTINGUISHING FEATURES: Animals such as eagles, wolves and grizzly bears are often used to represent families on totem poles.

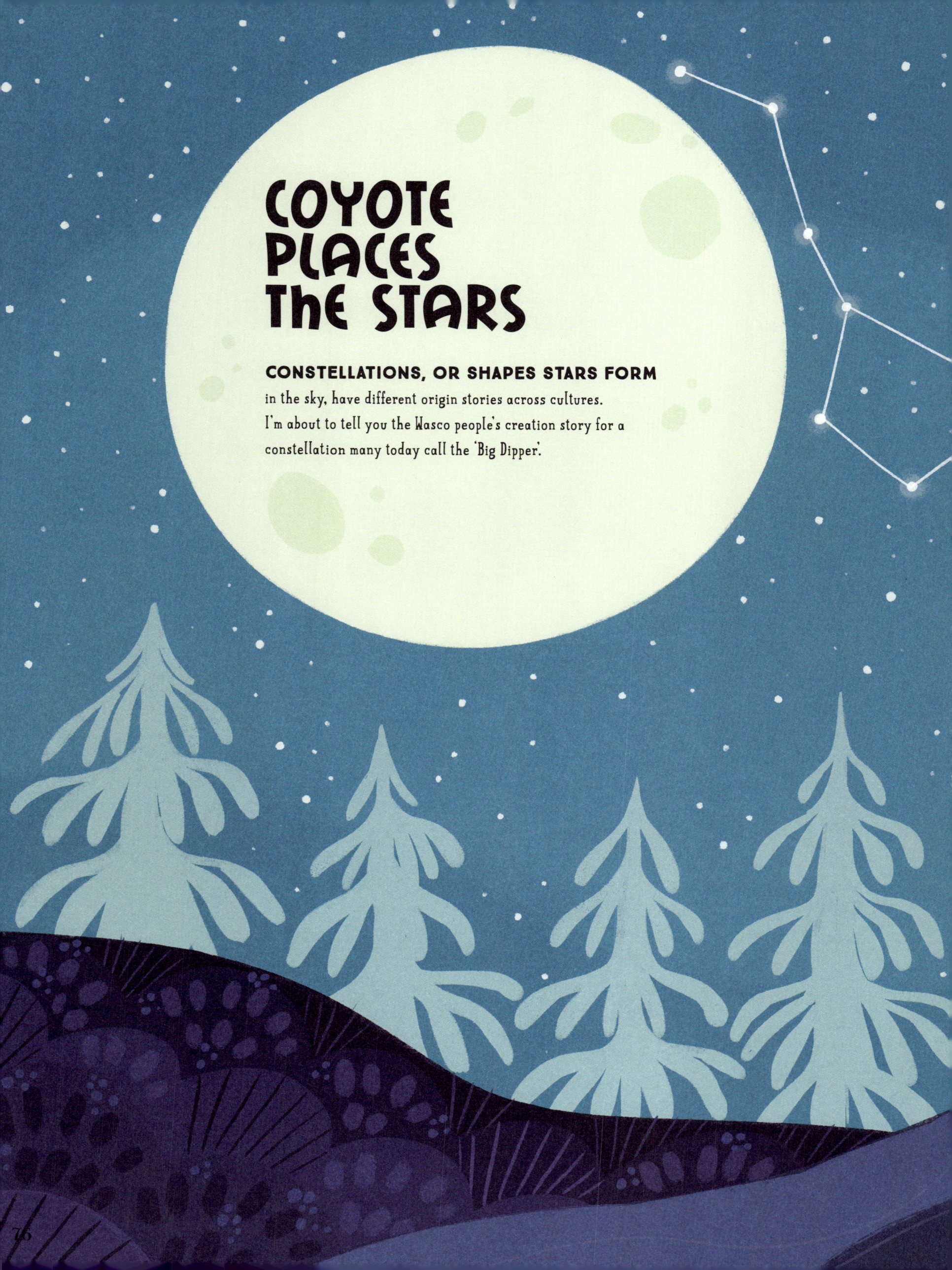

COYOTE PLACES THE STARS

CONSTELLATIONS, OR SHAPES STARS FORM in the sky, have different origin stories across cultures. I'm about to tell you the Wasco people's creation story for a constellation many today call the 'Big Dipper'.

ONCE, THERE WERE five wolf brothers who shared their meat with Coyote. Coyote noticed them looking at the sky and asked what they saw. The brothers told him they spotted two animals up there, but they could not get to them.

So Coyote shot arrows into the sky to form a ladder for him and the five brothers to climb. One of the brothers brought his dog on the journey.

When they had reached the sky, they saw the animals were grizzly bears. The wolves befriended the bears, and Coyote thought that they looked nice together. So he left them there, and took his ladder of arrows so they could not come down.

Today, when you look up in the night sky, the eight stars that make up the Big Dipper are the wolf brothers, the dog and the two grizzly bears.

CROW BRINGS DAYLIGHT

A VERY DETERMINED bird called Crow is the protagonist in this story from the Inuit people.

A LONG TIME AGO, the far north was completely dark. The Inuit people believed it was dark everywhere, but Crow told them that he had seen daylight. Excited, they asked the bird to bring it to them.

So Crow flew for many days until he found daylight. On the banks of the river near a village, he saw the daughter of the chief. Crow turned himself into a speck of dust and floated down to the girl's cloak.

When the girl returned to the chief's lodge, Crow saw a box with a glowing light within it. He floated over to the chief's young grandson, who was also there, and whispered, "Tell your grandfather you want to play with a ball of daylight." So the boy did.

The chief took the ball of daylight out of the box, tied it to a string and handed it to his grandson. At Crow's suggestion, the grandson took it outside. That's when Crow changed into his bird form again, snatched the ball of daylight and flew back to the north.

And that is how Crow brought daylight to the Inuit people.

MARZIA ACCATINO was born in Valenza, Italy in 1982. She attained a degree in communication science and a masters in multimedia communication. After a few years of working with Italian publishers, Marzia dedicated herself to becoming a nursery school teacher and studied for a degree in Primary Education. Thanks to a collaboration with White Star Kids, she has embraced publishing again and has successfully merged her two greatest passions: children's education and books.

LAURA BRENLLA may have formally started learning how to draw at the age of 16, but she grew up holding a pencil. She won a scholarship to study fine arts at the Universidad Europea, in Madrid, and, following graduation she spent two years specialising in animation. Later she was selected for digital clean-up training at the prestigious animation studio SPA, under the supervision of Fernando Moro. During this time, she developed strong drawing skills. Over the past few years, she has illustrated several books for White Star Kids.

ACKNOWLEDGMENTS

Author: Marzia Accatino / Illustrator: Laura Brenlla

Published in August 2020 by Lonely Planet Global Limited
CRN: 554153
ISBN: 978-1-83869-060-1
www.lonelyplanetkids.com

Printed in Italy
10 9 8 7 6 5 4 3 2 1

All rights reserved. No part of this publication may be reproduced, stored in a retrieval system, or transmitted in any form by any means, electronic, mechanical, photocopying, recording, or otherwise, except brief extracts for the purpose of review, without the written permission of the publisher. Lonely Planet and the Lonely Planet logo are trademarks of Lonely Planet and are registered in the US Patent and Trademark Office and in other countries.

Although the author and Lonely Planet have taken all reasonable care in preparing this book, we make no warranty about the accuracy or completeness of its content and, to the maximum extent permitted, disclaim all liability from its use.

STAY IN TOUCH - LONELYPLANET.COM/CONTACT

AUSTRALIA The Malt Store, Level 3, 551 Swanston St, Carlton, Victoria 3053 T: 03 8379 8000

IRELAND Digital Depot, Roe Lane (off Thomas St), Digital Hub, Dublin 8, D08 TCV4, Ireland

USA 155 Filbert Street, Suite 208, Oakland, CA 94607 T: 510 250 6400

UK 240 Blackfriars Rd, London SE1 8NW T: 020 3771 5100

WHITE STAR KIDS

White Star Kids® is a registered trademark property of White Star s.r.l.

© 2019 White Star s.r.l.
Piazzale Luigi Cadorna, 6
20123 Milan, Italy
www.whitestar.it